Game Boy

by

Alan Durant

Illustrated by Sue Mason

You do not need to read this page –
just get on with the book!

First published in 2004 in Great Britain by
Barrington Stoke Ltd
18 Walker Street, Edinburgh, EH3 7LP

www.barringtonstoke.co.uk

This edition published in 2007

Reprinted 2008

Copyright © 2004 Alan Durant
Illustrations © Sue Mason

ISBN: 978-1-84299-565-5

Printed in Great Britain by Bell & Bain Ltd

MEET THE AUTHOR – ALAN DURANT

What is your favourite animal?
Warthog
What is your favourite boy's name?
Buster
What is your favourite girl's name?
Bertha
What is your favourite food?
Brussel sprouts
What is your favourite music?
The hum of the central heating
on a frosty winter's morning
What is your favourite hobby?
Making things up

MEET THE ILLUSTRATOR – SUE MASON

What is your favourite animal?
Elephant
What is your favourite boy's name?
Dogboy Niffin (hello and thanks, you boys)
What is your favourite girl's name?
Weirdie (a special lady)
What is your favourite food?
Crumpets
What is your favourite music?
Reggae. From ska n' rocksteady
to dub plates n' ragga!
What is your favourite hobby?
Having a right old knees-up with
my cracking mates

For my nephew,
Frank Johnson,
as promised –
Alan Durant

For Jacks (and Marly) who helped me
on to the first rung of the ladder. X
And for Alsie Durant – thank you. X
Sue Mason

Contents

Level 1

JP held his left thumb down on the
controls of his GameBoy. His right thumb
twitched over the A button. The timing had
to be perfect or he'd end up in the pit of
deadly gunge.

NOW!

His right thumb jabbed down on the
button. On screen, Spaceman leapt and ...

made it! His hands grabbed the rock edge. His body and legs swung in the air.

But the danger wasn't over. An alien guard was marching up and down on the narrow rock above him.

The guard was armed with a splat gun. One blast from that gun and Spaceman was history.

Again, timing and speed were vital. Spaceman was up and standing the second the guard turned his back. A quick jab on button B and he was armed with a flame thrower.

The guard turned round. J P fired, once, twice, three times. Flames flew. The guard cried out and fell. A second later, he'd melted.

J P grinned. He loved zapping those aliens. In fact he loved zapping anything – aliens, snakes, dinosaurs, apes, whatever. If it moved, he'd zap it!

He pushed down on the controls again and sprinted to the end. Music blared out at him. A clock appeared on the screen, the hands spinning wildly. Then at last they stopped.

His time flashed up: two minutes, twenty-seven seconds! He'd done it! He'd beaten his record by four seconds. He didn't know anyone who had completed Level 7 of Alien Attack that fast. He was the champ!

He heard footsteps on the stairs. J P flicked the power switch to off. The machine gave a ping and went dead.

J P's mum put her head round the door. "You're supposed to be reading, John Paul," she said, "not playing with that thing." She nodded at the GameBoy.

"I wasn't playing with it," J P lied.

"Well, I can't see a book in your hand," his mum went on.

J P yawned. "I'm a bit tired tonight, Mum," he said. "I'll read tomorrow, I promise."

"Make sure you do," said Mum.

She turned out the light and kissed J P good night.

J P turned to the wall and smiled. He listened to his mum's footsteps going down the stairs. "Sorted," he said to himself.

Level 2

JP was cycling home from school the next day. The wind was at his back and he was racing down the hill towards the shops. He was really moving.

Suddenly a big, black cat ran out from between two parked cars right in front of JP. But JP didn't slow down. He yipped and shouted and rang his bell again and again. The cat got out of the way just in time. It shot under another parked car.

JP braked and got off his bike to look at the cat. It was shaking and looked scared stiff. Its tail was fluffed up to an enormous size.

"Silly cat," JP laughed. "You nearly got yourself zapped."

When JP looked up, his eyes widened with surprise. There was a new shop in the small shopping parade. It hadn't been there the last time JP had passed. But it looked as old as anything. Its window was full of junk, a battered tape player, a cracked vase, a broken chair, dusty plates, a scattering of boxless CDs ...

Something caught JP's eye. He wheeled his bike over to take a closer look. Yes, there, next to a rusty toaster was a GameBoy game. And what's more, it was one he'd never seen before! He thought he'd seen every game ever made, but not this one.

JP went into the shop. There was an old guy behind the counter. He was bald, except for a small, perfect cone of white hair on top of his head. He stared at JP through thick glasses that made his eyes look huge. They were odd eyes too. They gleamed in the middle like someone was shining a light into them.

JP felt a bit spooked, but he tried not to let the man see. "I'd like to have a look at that GameBoy game in the window," he said. "I've never seen one like it before. Is it an import?"

The man's eyes seemed to get even bigger. "You could say that," he said with an air of mystery. "But it's not a game. It's a real experience."

"Oh, right," JP laughed. "What's it called, this experience?"

"Call it what you want," said the man. "Some call it life, some call it death. It all depends upon how good a player you are." He smiled, showing a row of silver-capped teeth.

This guy is real weird, thought J P. "What do you mean?" he asked.

"You'll see," said the man. "I take it you wish to buy."

"Too right," said J P. "How much are you asking for it?"

They agreed a price. J P paid and was on his way. He was glad to be out of that shop too. That old guy had given him the creeps.

Level 3

JP went up to his room the moment he got home. His mum was making tea down in the kitchen. That meant she wouldn't bother him for a while.

He looked at the game. It had no picture or name on it. All it had was one line of print. It said: WARNING! THIS EXPERIENCE MAY SERIOUSLY DAMAGE YOUR HEALTH.

JP shook his head. This was a strange game. He was dying to find out what it was all about.

He got his GameBoy down from the shelf and loaded the game. He flicked the switch and the machine came to life with a ping. A message flashed on to the screen. It said: WARNING! ONCE YOU START, THERE IS NO GOING BACK!

JP laughed. You'd think the makers didn't want you to play. He pressed the start switch. Heavy, deep music growled from the speaker. Dum dum dum dum dum, dum dum! Dum dum dum dum dum, dum dum! This was more like it.

The screen showed a figure standing in a hot desert. In front of him were some kind of ruins. JP glanced around to see if there was a weapon for him to pick up. Yes, there, gleaming by a rock – a big dagger. JP pressed the control button and the figure ran forward. He bent down and picked up the dagger.

Good, now he was armed. JP hoped that there would be a gun too for him to pick up – maybe at the next level. Then he could do some serious zapping. He pressed the B button to put the dagger away, then pressed the controls and the figure ran on.

He climbed a pile of rocks and jumped down. He was in among the ruins now. He ran on. A tall, sheer rock blocked his way. No problem. A flick of the controls and the figure was bent double and rolling.

He went through a tunnel and out the other side. Then he was on his feet again. There was a yellow, spiky bush in front of him, blocking his way.

J P smiled. These were the moments he loved. He pressed button B and the dagger flashed on the screen. He pressed button A and the dagger slashed at the bush. Whomp, whomp, whomp! Three layers of bush were cut away. He crouched and slashed at the bush again. Whomp! No more bush! He put the dagger away, grinned and moved on.

He climbed up more rocks, jumped and rolled, on and on ...

J P was starting to feel let down. It was all too easy. He'd played much harder games than this. Where were the dangers?

Whoa! He stopped just in time. Right ahead of him, rising from under a rock, was a two-headed snake. It flicked its head at him and hissed. Another step and he'd have been dead. And he didn't fancy going all the way back to the start.

The snake hissed again. The sun beat down. JP could feel the sweat on his forehead. His hand was clammy as it closed round the dagger.

Hold on. Run that again.

His hand closed round the dagger. *His* hand. J P looked down. He looked up. He was standing among the ruins under the bright sun. In front of him a two-headed snake was hissing. But not on a screen – it was really there. And so was he.

"Wh-what?" he stuttered. What was going on? He was in his bedroom playing with his GameBoy. But he wasn't. He was part of the game, playing it from the inside!

JP took a step forward then leapt back as the snake almost got him. The near miss brought him to his senses. He took a bold step forward as the snake drew back. He braced himself and lifted the dagger to strike. As the snake's heads flicked again, he slashed quickly, once, twice. Whomp, whomp! The heads fell off and the snake vanished.

JP walked on, with great care, through an archway ... and everything went black.

Level 4

A moment later it was light again.
The ruins had gone. He was on a large, flat
stone at the edge of a swampy river.

"I must have come to the end of the level,"
he said to himself. He wondered what his
time had been. *It must have been good*, he
thought.

J P sat up on the stone to think. It seemed
to him that the game in his GameBoy was a

kind of simulator. It had the power to make the world of the game real. He had no idea how. Maybe there was some secret signal in the screen? Or perhaps it was passed through his fingers touching the control buttons. Whatever it was, it was amazing.

So this is what the man in the shop had meant when he said it was an experience. It was a bit over the top, though, to call it life or death. It was still only a game – even if it was a fantastic one.

Well, he was ready for the next level. It was time to move on.

J P looked out at the scene in front of him. There were different paths through the swamp, marked by logs and stones. There were sure to be hidden dangers too, so he'd have to be on his toes.

Croak! Something screeched above him, making him jump. A vulture-like bird with a long, sharp beak, swooped by him, too close for comfort. JP started to run.

He chose a sturdy-looking stone to begin crossing the swamp. He leapt forward to another. Then sideways. Then forward again – and to the left. So far, so good.

He considered the way ahead. He had a choice, one of three stones or a log. He decided against the log. It was half under the swamp and didn't look very safe. One of the stones was covered in green, mossy stuff and might be slippery. So that was out. That left two stones to choose from, one to the left, one to the right. Eeny, meeny, miney, mo.

The one to the right looked flatter. OK. He took a small step and jumped.

Bump!

Slosh!

Argh!

The stone sank beneath J P. The swamp sucked at his feet and ankles. It was like someone was under there grabbing him and pulling him down.

J P wobbled and struggled, trying to drag himself free – but the swamp was too strong. It was going to pull him under. He felt a rush of panic. He had to get free!

The swamp was round his knees now and was rising. There was only one chance. The log was just within reach. If he threw himself forward he could just about get his hands on it.

It didn't look very safe but he had no choice. The swamp tugged at his legs. He fell forward, reaching for the log.

He felt the rough bark scrape his hands as he grabbed it and pulled as hard as he could.

It was a desperate tug-of-war. At first he thought the swamp was winning, but slowly he eased his body up onto the log and his legs followed. At last his ankles and feet popped free. J P lay face down on the log, gasping.

After a while, J P was able to sit up. He was damp and covered in mud, but apart from that he was fine. The swamp hadn't got him, that was the important thing. He should have chosen this log to move on to in the first place, he thought. He'd have to be more careful next time.

He got to his feet slowly. He was over halfway across the swamp. There was a line of logs that looked as if they'd take him the rest of the way. But could he trust them?

Well, surely nothing could be worse than what had just happened to him. And he was still alive. He smiled. What did he have to lose? It was only a game after all.

He jumped onto the next log, walked along it and jumped again. Three logs, four logs ...

He was on a roll. This was pips – as easy as, well, falling off a log! There were only two to go and then he'd be there, another level completed. He jogged along the log, prepared to jump, when ...

Hold on!

He stopped, almost tipped forward, but just managed to keep his balance. Something about the next log worried him. He was sure it had moved. It was just a small quiver in the water, but a movement all the same.

JP gazed hard at the log, waiting to see if it moved again. It didn't.

But JP was wary. He didn't want another disaster like the sinking stone. He bent down and ripped a large piece of bark from the log he was standing on. He threw it through the air. It splashed in the water just in front of the log.

Whoosh!

JP shrank back in terror, as a set of giant teeth snapped through the water and shattered the bark. In a second the teeth had gone again, leaving a whirl of water.

But JP knew only too well what he'd seen: a wide snout, powerful jaws, dark hooded eyes – the log wasn't a log at all. It was a crocodile!

JP had a problem, a big problem. The log he was standing on was starting to sink. And what was worse, there were only two places he could move to – back to the stone that had sunk under him (it had risen to the surface again now) or forward to the crocodile.

After his moment of terror, J P felt quite cool. He'd faced problems like this lots of times before, playing his GameBoy.

He quickly made up his mind what he was going to do. If he jumped, then sprinted the moment he landed, he was sure he could get past the croc and on to the next log. After that, one leap and he'd be at the end of the level. And if he got it wrong, well, like he'd told himself before, it was only a game …

He was really up for this. His heart was pumping. He took two steps back on the sinking log, paused, put his head down and charged. Timing was vital. He needed to leave his leap to the last minute if he was going to clear the croc's head.

One, two, three, four, five, six, seven ...

Geronimo!!!!!

J P landed on the croc's back and ran for his life. The croc squirmed under him.

J P jumped again, feeling the snap of jaws at the back of his legs.

He didn't look back. J P was over the final log in a flash and on to the large, flat stone that marked the end of the swamp. He yelled and raised his arms in victory. "Result!" he cried.

Everything went black.

Level 5

Birds twittered. A monkey screeched. Further away, something roared.

J P looked around him. He was in a jungle – and it was hot. Already his face was damp with sweat. The back of his right leg felt sweaty too.

He looked down ... and gasped.

It wasn't sweat, it was blood! There was a jagged hole in his trousers and a gash on his leg. The croc's teeth must just have caught him as he made his escape.

So in this game, it seemed, you really could bleed. J P wished he could have seen the graphics. They must have been really cool.

The gash wasn't very deep, but sweat was trickling into it, making it sting. J P ripped a strip of cloth from his torn trousers and tied it round the gash.

Yes, that felt better. Something was puzzling him, though. OK, he'd been wounded by the croc. But that was on the last level. This was a new level. By any normal GameBoy rules, he should be fine. But then he should have realised by now, shouldn't he, that this was no ordinary game – it was an experience. Well, J P wanted more!

JP started to walk into the jungle, taking care to look out for dangers. He brushed aside huge leaves and pushed through thick bushes. He used his dagger to hack a path when the jungle got really thick.

It was hot work. JP had to keep wiping the sweat out of his eyes to see clearly. Once he nearly fell into a deep pit, but saw it just in time and jumped across. He couldn't see what was at the bottom of the pit, but he could hear lots of hissing and was sure there were snakes in there. He carried on into the jungle. He jumped over another pit full of sharp spikes. Then he grabbed hold of a vine and swung himself over another pit. He was starting to really enjoy himself.

Squawk! Squawk!

JP looked up to see a large parrot perched on the branch of a tree. Then his gaze fell on something else – something hanging

from the tree. It was bright purple and shaped like a diamond. It had a stem and seemed to be growing on the tree like some kind of strange fruit. But strangest of all was the fact that it was the only one on the whole tree.

Now J P had played enough games to know that there was usually something to collect as you passed through each level. It might be a flag, or a coin, or a health pack to help you get through harmful situations. This fruit was probably like that. Anyway, he wanted to get a closer look.

He studied the tree to see how he could get up into it. The trunk looked too smooth for climbing, but one of the branches was hanging down quite low. If he sprang up and grabbed it, he might be able to pull himself up. It was worth a try.

He ran forward, jumped and grabbed hold of the branch. For a few seconds he swung in the air, legs flapping, then he dragged himself up and up.

At last he found himself on a firm branch, with the diamond fruit just above him. Its skin was very smooth and shiny. JP reached up to touch it.

Squawk!

JP almost fell off his branch. He thought the parrot was going to peck him. But it didn't. It just sat on its branch glaring at him with its big, beady eyes.

JP grinned. "What's the matter with you, Polly?" he said. "You don't want me to take your fruit?" He shook his head. "Well, I'm sorry, but that's the game."

He reached up again, thinking this time he'd pick the fruit.

Squawk!

JP just smiled. Any moment, he'd have that smooth, shiny, purple diamond fruit in his hand and there was nothing the parrot could do to stop him. He just had to stretch a little more …

SQUAWK!

"Yah!" JP's fingers touched something hairy. A sharp pain shot through his hand. There was a large spider on the diamond fruit and it had bitten him. JP was annoyed with himself. He should have been ready for the danger.

JP's annoyance quickly turned to worry. The spider looked like a tarantula, which meant he was in big trouble. Already his hand was swelling and turning purple from the poison.

He was starting to feel sick. He remembered what the man in the shop had said about the game: "Some call it life, some call it death. It depends how good a player you are." Well, J P was good – and now he was going to have to prove it.

He knew for sure that he had only one chance to save himself: he had to get that fruit. But could he move fast enough?

He reached up with his other hand, making sure it was out of the spider's range. His whole body was flooded with sweat now from the heat and the worry and the poison that was seeping through him.

J P waited … Now! As the spider crawled out of view, J P made his move, snatching the fruit and slamming it against the branch.

Half of the fruit was squashed but so was
the spider. J P had zapped it!

"Result," he muttered weakly.

JP took a deep, shaky breath, closed his eyes and bit into the purple diamond fruit.

"Ah," he sighed as he felt the sweet fruit sooth and refresh him, getting rid of the poison.

Then he fell out of the tree.

Level 6

JP was in some kind of cave. There were flaming torches on the walls. In front of him the cave split into two tunnels. Which one should he choose: the right or the left? He'd chosen to go right in the swamp; so this time he went left.

JP took one of the torches off the wall and walked into the tunnel. He couldn't see very far ahead, so he went slowly. Who could say what might be waiting for him in the darkness? He'd had plenty of nasty surprises so far – maybe in this level he'd get a nice one. Nah, he didn't really believe that. It wasn't the way *this* game worked.

JP walked for a long time. But apart from a few cracks in the ground that he almost stumbled over, the tunnel had no dangers. It didn't lead anywhere either. It came to a dead end.

JP sat down to rest. He was tired and his bad leg was hurting. For the first time he thought about home and his bed and how nice it would be to find himself there. This was a cool game, but how many more levels were there? When would he reach the end?

After a while, JP got up again and walked back along the tunnel into the cave. Now there was only one way to go.

Let's hope this way leads somewhere, he thought to himself. He knew he wasn't going to get the best time for this level. He must have been down here for ages.

JP went a little faster down the right tunnel than he had down the left. He didn't like this dark world much and was keen to get out of it. The swamp and the jungle had been a lot more fun – even with the croc and the spider. This level was just, well, dull.

Rumble, rumble!

Maybe he'd spoken too soon. The ground started to shake under his feet. There was a booming sound in his ears. He walked a little slower, holding the flaming torch well in front of him. The noise got louder and louder. The shaking got stronger and stronger. What could it be? JP took out his dagger just to be on the safe side.

And then he saw it. It was enormous: a giant ant-like creature that filled the tunnel from top to bottom, side to side. Each move of its feet shook the ground. It glared down at JP with huge, red eyes. Then it opened its mouth.

JP cried out and fell back. The giant ant had teeth like knives.

The ground shook again as the thing moved towards JP. His heart was beating like a crazy drum. The dagger slipped from his hand and clinked on the floor. A picture came into his head of that big, black cat he'd nearly zapped. Well, now he knew how that cat felt. He was scared out of his wits.

He'd had enough of this game. He didn't want to play anymore. He wanted to be back in his room, with the GameBoy at his fingertips. And for a second he wondered who was at the GameBoy's controls. But he had more important things to worry about. The giant ant thing was coming closer and closer. Any moment now it was going to zap him! He had to do something. Think, J P, think!

J P glimpsed something behind the huge ant. It was a door. That must be the end of the level! He had to reach it. The ant was almost on him.

If you were playing the GameBoy, J P, what would you do? he asked himself. *Of course, you'd roll!*

Quick as a flash, J P crouched down. Then he rolled for his life. He rolled between the thing's tree-like legs and under its vast body – and then he was in front of the door. J P pulled the handle, heart racing. The door opened. He went through.

Once again, everything went black.

Level 7

JP looked around him. He was in a large room. It was full of walkways on different levels with lots of ladders to climb. It was like a life-size game of snakes and ladders – only without the snakes.

Well, that's what JP hoped anyway. He'd had enough of snakes and spiders and giant ants. Still, there was bound to be some sort of danger, he was sure of that.

At the far end of the room, on a high platform, were three large books. There was a huge message in bright lights above the books. It said simply *THE END*.

J P smiled. This was it – at last he'd reached the final level. Very soon he'd be at the end and then he could escape from this crazy game. He set off, climbing the nearest ladder.

There were more dangers, of course. But he was ready for them. They weren't creatures this time, but trap doors hidden in the walkways. They were hard to spot but J P was very careful. Once he did put his foot on a trapdoor, but was able to pull it back quickly when the door dropped open so he didn't fall through.

The near miss made him even more careful. There could only have been 50 metres at the most between the door to the room and the books, but it took J P ages.

He didn't want to make a mess of things now he was so near the end.

JP was in a kind of maze. Many of the walkways led nowhere and he had to turn and try another way. This happened time and again. But, at last, he was at the foot of the tall ladder that would take him up to the platform where the books were.

He climbed up with eager hands ...

The platform was smaller than he'd thought it would be. There was just enough room for him and the books.

Each book rested on a golden stand. JP stepped onto the platform and a red light flashed above him.

A new message appeared under the words *THE END*.

One of these three
books contains true
wisdom and is worth
its weight in gold.
The others are false
and worth nothing.
Which will you choose?
But beware, choose
wrong and you die!
You have one minute
to make up your mind.
Good luck.
You will need it.

The message vanished. A clock appeared in its place and its hand started to move round.

As J P watched, ten seconds went by. He had to act fast.

J P stared at the books, one after another. The first was splendid. Its cover was gold and was set with diamonds, rubies and pearls. It must be worth a fortune, J P thought.

He looked at the second book. It was made of tiger skin with a spine of white ivory. Like the first book, it looked as if it must be worth a lot of money.

His eyes moved on to the third book. Well, this one didn't look much at all. The cover was plain red cardboard and tatty – it was the kind of book you might find at a car boot sale or in a junk shop. It couldn't be worth more than a few pence.

He glanced back at the clock. Thirty seconds had gone. Only thirty seconds left ...

JP looked again at the three books. It had to be the book with all the jewels. Of course that was worth its weight in gold. It was simple! He stepped towards it ... then stopped.

It was too simple. A thought came into his head – something his mum often said: *Never judge a book by its cover.*

Forty seconds gone ...

JP's palms were damp with sweat. His heart was pumping again.

Forty-five seconds gone ...

Not the book with the jewels then. It must be the second book with the tiger skin. He put one hand out to touch it, then stopped again. Tiger skin. Ivory. Things stolen from murdered animals.

JP liked zapping things in his GameBoy games, but he knew that killing real tigers and elephants was wrong. They were endangered animals. How could any book covered in tiger skin and ivory contain true wisdom?

Fifty seconds ...

JP hesitated. It couldn't be the third book. Surely, not the third book.

Fifty-two seconds ...

Look at it. It wasn't worth anything. It was junk.

Fifty-four seconds ...

Junk! JP's brain sparked into life.

Fifty-six seconds ...

Where did this game come from? It came from a junk shop!

Fifty-eight seconds ...

But the book was so tatty!

Fifty-nine seconds ...

He had to choose.

This was it then. He was going to die!

JP took a step forward and opened the third book ...

The red light flashed again. The clock vanished. The golden book and the tiger skin book burst into flames and vanished too. The platform slid away.

JP dropped like a stone down into the dark.

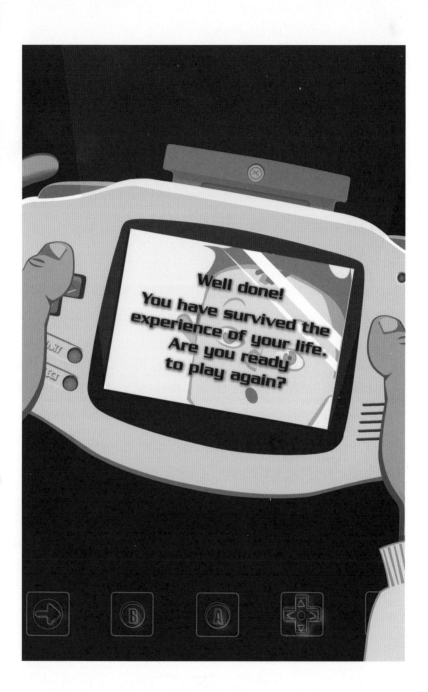

Level 8

JP's thumbs were on the control buttons. His eyes were gazing at the screen and the message that was there: "Well done! You have survived the experience of your life. Are you ready to play again?"

"No fear," JP muttered. He flicked the switch and turned his GameBoy off. Then he lay back on his bed and took a deep breath. His heart was pumping and his whole body

was trembling. That game had really shaken him up.

He thought about that last level. He'd made the right choice, but what if he'd chosen one of the other books? Then the flames would have got him too, wouldn't they? He'd be dead now. Really dead. Or had it all been a game? Well, whatever, it was much too real for his liking. He had no wish ever to play it again. In fact, he was going to take it back to the shop right now.

JP glanced at his watch. He must have been away for hours, he thought. But he hadn't. He was amazed to discover that no time had passed at all. He could hear his mum downstairs getting tea ready.

JP took the game out of the GameBoy and hurried downstairs.

"Mum, I'm just going up to the shops," he called. "I'll be back in a few minutes."

He ran out of the house without waiting for a reply.

He ran all the way to the shopping parade, taking the short cut past the canal. There were lots of questions he wanted to ask that weird guy in the junk shop: How did the game work? Were there others like it? Who made it and how did they make it so real?

But JP never got the chance to ask his questions. When he arrived at the shopping parade he was amazed to find that the shop had gone. Well, it was empty anyway. There was a sign outside that read, FOR SALE.

JP went into the newspaper shop.

"Excuse me, do you know what happened to the junk shop next door?" he asked the shopkeeper.

The man gave him a funny look. "There's no junk shop next door," he said. "That place has been empty for weeks."

JP frowned. How could that be true?

JP walked home, deep in thought. The whole thing was weird, he decided: the junk shop, the man with the odd cone of hair, the game that called itself an experience ... No, it was more than weird; it was creepy, scary.

JP looked at the game in his hand and he shivered. He wanted to be rid of the thing, but he didn't want anyone else to have it. It was too dangerous. He needed to put it somewhere where it couldn't do any harm, where it couldn't tempt anyone and zap them ... He knew the perfect place.

He walked down to the canal and on to the narrow, stone footbridge that crossed it. He took one last look at the strange, deadly game in his hand, then threw it out into the canal. It plopped into the water with a small splash and was gone. JP stood for a moment or two, gazing down. Then he turned and ran home for tea.

JP didn't play his GameBoy that night. He read a book instead. It was an old book his mum had bought him at a car boot sale. It had a rubbish cover, but the story was good. It was really exciting.

But not too exciting.

Barrington Stoke would like to thank all its readers for commenting on the manuscript before publication and in particular:

Annabel Ashworth	Louise Marshall
Erin Laura Barry	Lynsey Martin
Christine Bilham	Lizzy McCaffrey
William Branton	Rosy McCaffrey
Grant Brown	Brendan Pollitt
Louis Brown	Andrew Reynolds
Max Carpanini	Kirsty Roebuck
David De Min	George Saunders
Andrew Dove	Isobel Stanton
Kyra Gaunt	Laura Thompson
Madeleine Howie	Xandie Trevor
Jonny Jones	Greg Turnbull
Angus Kunkler	Mrs Greta Walker
Mrs D. Leddy	Calum Wallace

Become a Consultant!

Would you like to give us feedback on our titles before they are published? Contact us at the email address or website below – we'd love to hear from you!

Email: info@barringtonstoke.co.uk
Website: www.barringtonstoke.co.uk

If you liked this,
why don't you try?

Game Boy Reloaded
by Alan Durant

Mia and Zak find a strange games console in the canal. When you play it, it sucks you inside the game. But now Zak's vanished. Can Mia save him? Or will they both be trapped forever?

The action-packed sequel to *Game Boy*.

You can order *Game Boy Reloaded* directly from our website at www.barringtonstoke.co.uk